AN AFRICAN STORY

A Promise to the Sun

by Tololwa M. Mollel ❖ Illustrated by Beatriz Vidal

Little, Brown and Company
Boston Toronto London

First Edition

Library of Congress Cataloging-in-Publication Data

Mollel, Tololwa M. (Tololwa Marti)
    A promise to the sun : an African story / by Tololwa M. Mollel ;
illustrated by Beatriz Vidal. — 1st ed.
        p.   cm.
    Summary: Explains why bats come out of their caves only at night.
    ISBN 0-316-57813-4 (lib. bdg.)
    [1. Bats — Fiction. 2. Africa — Fiction.] I. Vidal, Beatriz, ill.
II. Title.
PZ7.M7335PR   1992
[E] — dc20   90-13326

Joy Street Books are published by
Little, Brown and Company (Inc.)

10 9 8 7 6 5 4 3 2

LB

Published simultaneously in Canada
by Little, Brown & Company (Canada) Limited

Printed in the United States of America

The paintings in this book were done in mixed media —
watercolor, acrylic, and crayon.

To my son Emeka
T. M.

A mi querida Madre, in memoriam
B. V.

Long ago, when the world was new, a severe drought hit the land of the birds. The savannah turned brown, and streams dried up. Maize plants died, and banana trees shriveled in the sun, their broad leaves wilting away. Even the nearby forest grew withered and pale.

The birds held a meeting and decided to send someone in search of rain. They drew lots to choose who would go on the journey. And they told the Bat, their distant cousin who was visiting, that she must draw, too. "You might not be a bird," they said, "but for now you're one of us." Everyone took a lot, and as luck would have it, the task fell to the Bat.

Over the trees and the mountains flew the Bat, to the Moon. There she cried, "Earth has no rain, Earth has no food, Earth asks for rain!"

The Moon smiled. "I can't bring rain. My task is to wash and oil the night's face. But you can try the Stars."

On flew the Bat, until she found the Stars at play. "Away with
you!" they snapped, angry at being interrupted. "If you want
rain, go to the Clouds!"

The Clouds were asleep but awoke at the sound of the Bat arriving. "We can bring rain," they yawned, "but the Winds must first blow us together, to hang over the Earth in one big lump."

At the approach of the Bat, the Winds howled to a stop.
"We'll blow the Clouds together," they said, "but not before
the Sun has brought up steam to the sky."

As the Bat flew toward the Sun, a sudden scream shook the sky: "Stop where you are, foolish Bat, before I burn off your little wings!" The Bat shrank back in terror, and the Sun smothered its fire in rolls of clouds. Quickly the Bat said, "Earth has no rain, Earth has no food, Earth asks for rain!"

"I'll help you," replied the Sun, "in return for a favor. After the rain falls, choose for me the greenest patch on the forest top, and build me a nest there. Then no longer will I have to journey to the horizon at the end of each day but will rest for the night in the cool and quiet of the forest."

The Bat quickly replied, "I'm only a Bat and don't know how to build nests, but the birds will happily make you one. Nothing will be easier — there are so many of them. They will do it right after the harvest, I promise — all in a day!"

And down the sky's sunlit paths the Bat flew, excited to bring the good news to the birds.

The birds readily promised to build the nest.

"The very day after the harvest," said the Sparrow.

"All in a day," said the Owl.

"A beautiful nest it'll be," said the Canary.

"With all the colors of the rainbow!" said the Peacock.

So the Sun burnt down upon the earth, steam rose, Winds blew, and Clouds gathered. Then rain fell. The savannah bloomed, and streams flowed. Green and thick and tall, the forest grew until it touched the sky. Crops flourished and ripened — maize, bananas, cassava, millet, and peanuts — and the birds harvested.

The morning after the harvest, the Bat reminded the birds about the nest. Suddenly the birds were in no mood for work. All they cared about was the harvest celebrations, which were to start that night and last several days.

"I have to adorn myself," said the Peacock.

"I have to practice my flute," said the Canary.

"I have to heat up my drums," said the Owl.

"I have to help prepare the feast," said the Sparrow.

"Wait until after the celebrations," they said. "We'll do it then." But their hearts were not in it, and the Bat knew they would never build the nest.

What was she to do? A promise is a promise, she believed, yet she didn't know anything about making a nest. Even if she did, how could she, all on her own, hope to make one big enough for the Sun?

The Sun set, and the Moon rose. The celebrations began.
The drums throbbed, the flutes wailed, and the dancers
pounded the earth with their feet.
Alone with her thoughts and tired, the Bat fell fast asleep.

She awoke in a panic. The Moon had vanished, the Stars faded. Soon the Sun would rise!

Slowly, the Sun peered out over the horizon in search of the nest. Certain the Sun was looking for her, the Bat scrambled behind a banana leaf. The Sun moved up in the sky. One of its rays glared over the leaf. With a cry of fear, the Bat fled to the forest.

But even there, she was not long at peace. There was a gust of wind, and the forest opened for a moment overhead. The Bat looked up anxiously. Peeking down at her was the Sun.

She let out a shriek and flew away.

As she flew, a cave came into view below. She dived down and quickly darted in.

There, silent and out of reach, she hid from the glare of the Sun. She hid from the shame of a broken promise, a shame the birds did not feel.

Outside, the celebrations went on. The Owl's drums roared furiously. The Canary's flute pierced the air. And the Sparrow cheered the Peacock's wild dancing.

The Sun inched down toward the horizon. It lingered over the forest and cast one more glance at the treetops, hoping for a miracle. Then, disappointed, it began to set. The birds carried on unconcerned, the sounds of their festivities reaching into the cave.

But the Bat did not stir from her hiding place that night. Nor the next day. For many days and nights she huddled in the cave. Then gradually she got up enough courage to venture out — but never in daylight! Only after sunset with Earth in the embrace of night.

Days and months and years went by, but the birds didn't build the nest. The Sun never gave up wishing, though. Every day as it set, it would linger to cast one last, hopeful glance at the forest top. Then, slowly, very slowly, it would sink away below the horizon.

Year after year the Sun continued to drag up steam, so the Winds would blow, the Clouds gather, and rain fall. It continues to do so today, hoping that the birds will one day keep their promise and build a nest among the treetops.

As for the Bat, . . .

. . . she made a home in the cave, and there she lives to this day.
Whenever it rains, though, she listens eagerly. From the dark silence
of her perch, the sound of the downpour, ripening the crops and
renewing the forest, is to her a magical song she wishes she could be
out dancing to.
And as she listens, the trees outside sway and bow toward the cave. It
is their thank-you salute to the hero who helped turn the forests green
and thick and tall as the sky.